I0699783

Working Blue Press

Master of the Bedroom.
Copyright © 2025 by Working Blue Press. All rights reserved. Printed in the United States of America. No part of this book may be used or reproduced in any manner without written permission except in the case of brief quotations embodied in critical articles and reviews. For permissions, information, and/or educational, business, or sales promotional use, please e-mail the marketing department at workingbluepress@gmail.com.

First Edition

ISBN 978-1-967038-12-1 (Kindle)
ISBN 978-1-967038-13-8 (Print)

For all the men and women who love
great sex, great relationships, and a
damn good time.

Content

Suggestions for Further Reading

Men Who Renovate Erotic Series
Books 1, 2, 3 and 4.

Follow Lacey Love on Amazon to keep abreast of new releases!

Master of the
Bedroom

Men Who Renovate Erotic Series

Book 1

1

Master of the Bedroom

Wolfe walked into the dusty, old office on the far side of town in Little Palace, North Carolina. It wasn't much, but it was cheap and served the purpose he and his three buddies needed.

"What's up?" Danny said as soon as Wolfe walked in. Danny was always dressed liked he just walked out of a North Face ad campaign and today was no exception with his dark blue jeans and hunter green jacket.

"I fucked the client," Wolfe spit out less eloquently than he intended.

Jack spit out his Dunkin' Donuts coffee as Ben dropped the *Playboy* magazine in his hands and looked at Wolfe like he was more interesting than the centerfold.

"I'm gonna need more information," Ben said. His grin was wide on his square face that was sporting some scruff to match his dark eyes and dark, spiked hair. His University of North Carolina football sweatshirt had its sleeves pulled up his forearms as he leaned his elbows on his knees.

"Are you talkin' about Gina?" Jack said, his green eyes laughing as he shifted in his worn blue jeans and propped his boots up on one of the old, metal cabinets. "The newly divorced hot, older chick with the master bedroom renovation?"

Wolfe nodded as he tossed his keys on his desk and turned back to three probing stares.

"I mean, we started this renovation side hustle so we could make some extra cash," Wolfe said. He ran his fingers through his

clean-cut dark hair, loose at the top.
"I wanna buy my own place.
We've all been out of college four
years. It's time to grow up. And
now…this. Shit."

"Did she pay you?" Jack asked.

"Yeah. Wait, for what? What do
you mean?" Wolfe asked.

"I mean, what did her money
pay for?" Ben asked with a laugh.

"She paid us for the renovation,
assholes," Wolfe said. "She paid it
upfront. Well before anything
happened."

"As long as we're not running a
gigolo service," Danny said with a
laugh. But Wolfe knew his friend
of twenty-one years better than
that. Danny meant what he said,
even if he delivered it with a smile.

"Yeah, I know," Wolfe said.
"It's not. It didn't happen like that."

"Good," Danny said.

"So, how did it happen?" Jack
asked.

"Yeah, we need details," Ben added. "What were you? Like the master of the bedroom?"

They all laughed as Wolfe sighed. "Alright, here's what went down."

2

Wolfe in Sheep's Clothing

Wolfe walked up to the front door of the six-bedroom, four-thousand square foot house and rang the bell. Gina was his first renovation client, and he was five minutes early. He wanted to make a good impression. If she referred more rich clients like her, they could all pay off their college loans, Wolfe could get himself a house, and his buddies could check off a few things on their wish lists, too.

It wasn't easy working a full-time job as a ticket salesperson at the local minor league hockey arena and then picking up small project renovation work on the side, but he figured after a couple years, he'd have the money he needed to buy that house on Cherry Lane. Hopefully this job and others like it would be the thing to get him exactly what he needed."

"Hi," a sexy voice said as the door swung open.

"Whoa," he uttered before he could stop it.

Gina-fucking-Byers. Good God. The woman was a vision with rich, mahogany colored hair and bright red lips. Her eyes were a light hazel and they stared at him with humor as he remained speechless. He couldn't help noticing her curves in those Yoga pants and scarlet red sports bra.

"You must be Wolfe," she said casually.

"Uh, yeah, I am," he said. *Get it together, dude.* "Wolfe Dagger. Dagger Renovations. Nice to meet you."

She grinned as she took his hand that he extended to her. The minute her soft skin touched his rough hand he wanted nothing more than to bend her over a table and slide deep inside her.

"Nice to meet you," she cooed. "Wolfe."

She turned inside the house and left the door open for him to follow, which he eagerly did. How the hell was he going to concentrate with her around? And in her bedroom no less.

"So, what is it exactly you'd like done, Mrs. Byers?" he asked as he followed her through the gorgeous home. Everything was high-end, decorated in creams and natural colors, comfortable fabrics that were good for fucking, and a top-shelf kitchen with everything stainless steel.

Her turned his attention to her firm backside as she laughed.

"Is that funny?" he asked.

"It's funny you called me Mrs.," she smarted as she walked up a staircase, her delicate fingers sliding along the rail. He could only imagine what those fingers might feel like sliding along his stiff shaft.

"Oh, I'm sorry," he said.

"It's okay," she said. She walked down the hallway of the second floor and turned into a door to her left. He followed her into a large bedroom with clean, natural furniture, but sparse decorations, a couple of toppled over picture frames, and only one side of the bed rumpled from sleep. There was a gas fireplace and a small sitting area. It was a gorgeous master bedroom.

"I'm divorced," she finally said with a sigh. "Finalized three days ago. And now, I need to…"

She paused as she looked him over with a seductive heat he felt in his bones. It was obvious that they shared a mutual desire for him to drive his cock deep inside her.

"Christen this room with something new."

He turned on the most seductive stare he could muster. He was used to this reaction from women. He was a quarterback in high school and college, good-looking—or so he was told—and chiseled from never-ending workouts. Even though he'd graduated four years ago, he still ran and worked out religiously, maintaining a strong physique. Women liked him. Women liked him to fuck them. And he had no problem with that. The problem was that she was a client.

He shut off his charm by clearing his throat and putting on

the best business face he could muster.

"Okay, sounds good," he said. He broke her heated stare and glanced around. "I think you mentioned new paint, tearing up this carpet and putting down hardwood floors, and something in the master bathroom?"

She grinned at him as she slid past him, leaving only a few centimeters even though there was at least three feet on either side of him.

"Follow me," she purred.

As she walked past him, he could smell her sweet scent and caught how beautiful and full her breasts were. Who was the idiot who left this goddess?

He followed her into the large bathroom and couldn't see where anything needed fixed, except maybe an updated shower.

"I want one of those rain showers," she said, as if reading his mind. "I like the way the water pounds my body."

He knew what she was getting at as her lips parted and she turned to face him, her nipples hard and rubbing against the fabric of her sports bra.

"It's definitely good for a massage," he said. Holy shit he wanted to fuck her in the shower. And the bed. And everywhere else in this damn house he could find. He cleared his throat again. "I can get you a quote later today. Do you know what color you want the walls painted?"

"I do," she said. She started to move toward him. "I've already picked out the materials. You just need to measure and go pick up what you need."

She stopped in front of him as her nipples just barely grazed his chest. His cock immediately responded, stiffening at her presence.

"Once I get your quote, I'll pay you immediately," she said. She trailed a fingertip up his forearm and an electric spark jolted his balls making him hard enough to start pushing against the fabric of his jeans. "Can you have it done by the end of the month?"

Her hazel eyes met his and his breath caught. She was absolutely fucking stunning and maybe in her late twenties or early thirties? Definitely old enough to know what she liked in bed and maybe even experiment a little bit.

"I can," he said.

She smiled as she slid her hand off his arm. "Good. Send me the quote, I'll pay, and then I'll see you two days from now to get started."

"Sounds good," he said. She turned and walked out as he

followed. He wasn't sure how he was going to keep his focus while he worked for her, but he would figure it out.

He needed this job to work. He needed her recommendation. And he needed to keep distance between them if he was going to get through this job without giving her every single naughty thing she wanted from him—and he wanted to give her.

3

Hand Towels

Wolfe was barely hanging on by a thread. He'd been working at Gina's house for two days and his balls were so blue he could barely walk.

"Wolfe," she cooed as she walked into the bathroom. "When can I take a shower?"

He glanced toward her from inside the tiled haven where he had already dismantled the previous equipment and was now installing the new rain shower head. His cock was immediately hard as he took in the hand towel she was using to cover only strategic portions of her body.

"In about an hour," he said. He wanted to take his eyes off her, but it was impossible. She was too damn beautiful, and he was too damn attracted to her to do much of anything except let the thrill of her practically naked body three feet from his take over. "Unless you're already wet."

He couldn't believe he'd let those words come out of his mouth, but he couldn't stand it anymore. She'd barely worn any clothing from the day he started, walking around in thin fabrics and no bra, her nipples always hard when she was near him. It drove him crazy. And now here she was, naked and wanting him.

And he wanted her, too.

"I'm soaking wet," she purred as she dropped the hand towel. He instantly moved toward her, going straight for those beautiful, pink nipples standing at attention and calling for his mouth.

"Oh God," she moaned as his tongue licked her right nipple then pulled it into his mouth and started sucking it. His hand found the other soft mound and his thumb caressed the pink nub. "Suck them both."

He moved from one nipple to the other as his hand slid down her body and found her slick opening. His fingers easily entered her folds as he lightly nipped her breasts.

"Fuck yes," she moaned. Her hands grabbed his hair as his fingers thrust in and out of her wetness. He needed to taste her. Everything about her smelled amazing and he imagined she tasted the same.

"God you're beautiful," he said. He let go of her nipple and kissed his way down her curvy, toned abs to her perfectly waxed pussy. He took a deep breath of her sexiness. "Fuck you smell good."

"Taste me," she groaned.

He grabbed her ass with his hands and buried his face between her legs, separating her lips with his tongue and taking her clit into his mouth. He rolled the little pink mound with lips and tongue, sucking and licking as she started to pant.

"Holy fuck, yes," she yelled as she gripped his hair.

He loved the feeling of her hands yanking on his mane as he tasted her sweetness. She was as he expected with a taste like honey and cinnamon or some kind of warm spice. He couldn't get enough of her as his tongue painted every surface of her slit.

"Fuck me," she panted.

He ran his hands up her body as he moved from her moist center up her body to her throat, sucking and kissing as he went. He picked her up by her tiny waist and set her on the sink.

"Spread your legs, beautiful," he said silkily as she obeyed. She already had his pants undone as he helped her slide them down.

"Fuck you're huge." He could tell she was pleased as she reached out with those delicate hands and started to stroke him. God he'd been waiting and wanting those cool hands on his cock for days now.

"Fuck yes," he moaned.

"You like that, baby?" she whispered.

"God yes," he panted. "I need to fuck you."

"Yes, baby." She pulled her hand away and balanced herself on the sink as she spread her legs wider.

"Fuck your pussy is amazing," he said as he ran his hands up and down her inner thighs, massaging her pussy and her breasts as she gave him all access.

"Oh yes," she moaned. "Fuck me now."

He did as he was told and teased her slick entrance with his wet tip. The precum shining as he tortured her with a slow push of his tip into her sweet mound.

"Oh fuck," she groaned.

"Baby, is that what you want?"

She nodded quickly as she panted, "Please, baby, fuck me!"

"Whatever you want." He grabbed her hips and quickly slid deep inside of her as they both moaned with intense pleasure.

"Holy shit, your cock is fucking huge," she yelled. "More, fuck me!"

"Fuck yes," he moaned. "Fuck."

He pounded her quick and fast, then slow and gentle, varying the pace and how deep he was, driving her crazy with pleasure.

"Oh baby," she moaned. Her head tipped back, her breasts fully exposed. He dipped down and sucked her titties as he thrust deep inside and held his cock firmly inside of her, giving her tiny little pulses right on her G-spot.

"How's that gorgeous?"

"I'm gonna fucking come," she moaned. "Harder!"

He stayed right where he was and pounded his length inside her, slamming his balls right against her ass to make her shudder.

"I'm coming!" she yelled with pleasure, her breasts bouncing as he felt his own orgasm rise to the occasion.

"Fuck, I'm coming, too," he yelled.

"Yes!

He pulled out and started giving her long, full thrusts, his balls banging her ass as his cock deeply sunk into her in powerful strides.

"I'm coming!" he yelled.

And they both writhed their hips against each other trying to push each other into powerful orgasms as the waves of pleasure washed over them. He could feel her wetness all over his cock and he loved it.

"Fuck," he said as he caught his breath. "Fuck, you're amazing."

They both laid there for a second as they started to breath normally again and their heart rates slowed.

"God you can fuck," she finally said. She grinned as he helped her off the sink to a standing position. He picked up the hand towel and handed it to her.

"Your towel." They both laughed at its tiny size.

"I wasn't too obvious, was I?" She winked.

"Maybe just a little," he said. "I didn't mind."

"So," she said as she leaned into his body again. "How long until this job is finished?"

"A few weeks," he said. He leaned down and kissed along her neck.

"Good," she said as she stepped away and smiled. "I have quite a few…private renovations for you to work on."

He grinned as she turned and walked out.

"Happy to help any way I can," he said.

She peered over her shoulder. "Trust me, you're the best help I've gotten in years."

He pulled up his pants and got dressed as he heard her get in the shower down the hall.

So much for staying focused on the job. But with her around, there was no way he was going to stick to just the work. He was definitely going to give her more than just a new bedroom.

4

Break the Bed

Gina was waiting for the opportunity to have Wolfe inside her again. Since the shower incident, he'd finished the bathroom, but he had to bring in extra help when she decided spur of the moment that she wanted new tile. A seafoam green that made the space more natural-looking. To stay on time, his co-owner Ben came to help for a few hours.

She had gone to hot Yoga at that point and stayed away while they finished. And for the last four days Wolfe had been at his regular job selling ticket packages to fat cats like her ex-husband, Blaine. Now Wolfe was back and repainting her bedroom. He'd started a few hours ago and he was almost done with the first coat. The windows were wide open, and the fresh summer air was clearing out the paint fumes.

She glanced at herself in the mirror of the bathroom down the hall. She'd spent time poolside this week, tanning her skin in anticipation of his hands all over her body again. Her dark hair was shimmering as it cascaded over her full breasts. She touched them now and let out a soft sigh as her fingers pinched and caressed her nipples.

"Mmmm," she murmured.

Wolfe was exactly what she needed right now. The pain from her divorce was still a dull ache in her gut after she found her husband in bed with a local Kindergarten teacher fresh out of college. They were living together now and the twenty-four-year-old was already pregnant.

"No," she whispered as the tears hit her eyes. "Don't."

She had cried enough over Blaine and their failed marriage. She'd shed as many tears as she was willing to over the two miscarriages she'd suffered and the silent torture she put herself through after. She had shut Blaine out of her misery and carried the weight alone. She had been the one to refuse therapy and eventually it was enough to drive him away.

They had both been assholes. She knew that. In hindsight she could see they never should have gotten married in the first place. They were high school sweethearts who outgrew each other in college but got married anyway because that's what they were supposed to do.

And now here she was. She was living in this big house—too big for just her—alone and starting her life over again at thirty years old. And what the hell did that look like? It created both a sense of exhilarating freedom and absolute terror, all at the same time.

She let out a slow exhale. Wolfe was a bright spot that was spurring her on and helping her feel alive again.

She reached out to touch the mirror as she traced the lines of her face in it. She smiled at her reflection.

"You're gonna be okay," she whispered.

She pulled her hand back and slid it up and down her body, then between her legs and slowly circled her clit with pleasure as she thought about Wolfe.

She had chosen his business because no one knew them. And in this small town, everybody knew everybody, and all the other contractors or small renovation businesses knew her ex-husband and wouldn't hesitate to tell him everything she was doing. Dagger Renovations had just opened and so she called on a whim.

She had thought Wolfe's voice was sexy, but she had no idea how hot he truly was until she opened the door and saw him the first day he came to give her the quote. After that, she couldn't stop thinking about him and having him between her legs.

It's exactly what she needed to help her in the final stretch of recovering from her divorce. And he didn't seem to mind helping.

"Oh God," she murmured. She had to stop touching herself or she'd come right there.

She looked at her heavy, sensual eyes in the mirror and knew her body was ready for him again. She left the bathroom and tip-toed down the hallway into the bedroom. She quietly crawled onto the bed, which was pulled away from the wall and stripped down to the mattress while he worked. She positioned herself on her knees, doggy-style, with her open, wet pussy facing him. She glanced over her shoulder.

"Wolfe?" she said gently. "Can you help me real quick?"

"Jesus," he said as he turned to her. Immediately his cock tried to burst of his jeans and she could see the desire on his face as he dropped his gear and slid his shirt off, then his pants, and work boots and socks. His cock was so thick and beautiful she could barely contain herself.

"Fuck me," she said urgently. "Please."

"Fuck, yes," he said.

He wasted no time taking the tip of his cock and circling it around her entrance as she moaned.

"Yes, baby, yes," she moaned. "Tease me."

"You like that?" he asked. He pushed just the tip in and out.

"God, yes," she panted. He was young, but he knew how to fuck. A guy like that would have had girls throwing themselves at him since he was in high school. He was no stranger to pussy or what it took to make a woman scream. "Tease me, baby."

He pulled his tip out and squeezed her hips as she protested.

"Put it back in," she begged.

"No," he said. "Not yet."

He dipped down to his knees on the bed and buried his face between her legs as he squeezed her ass roughly.

"Fuck yes!" she screamed. "Smack my ass, baby."

He did as he was told and gave her a strong slap that she felt deep in her core as his tongue found her clit and rubbed it erotically.

"Oh God, Wolfe, yes," she moaned.

"Fuck, you taste amazing," he said as he pulled back and then dove back in, driving his tongue inside her.

"Fuck!" she screamed as she leaned forward and gripped the mattress at the top of the bed, her nipples rubbing the hard satin of the firm foam. "Eat my ass, baby."

"Fuck yes," he moaned. She felt his tongue slip out of her slick folds and tease its way up to her tight, pink hole as he flicked it with pleasure. "Like that, baby?"

"Oh God, yes," she panted. "Smack my ass while you do it."

He slapped once, twice, three times, on her perfect ass as his tongue bathed her puckered hole in a delicious bath of pleasure.

"Oh God," she moaned. "I'm gonna come, baby."

"Come," he ordered as stopped to give her a hard slap and then dove back in as her orgasm reached the edge and tumbled over in waves of incredible pleasure.

"Fuck, I'm coming," she barely got out as the waves crashed over her.

"Fuck yes," he said. He stopped and lifted her hips, then drove his thick, hard cock into her wet pussy, slapping his balls against her clit as he thrust inside her. "Fucking come again with my cock in you, baby."

"Yes, baby, yes," she screamed. She could feel a second orgasm rising as he pounded her from behind, that thick cock slamming against her G-spot.

"You like that big cock fucking inside you?"

"Yes!"

"Yeah?" he pressed. "How much, baby? Tell me."

"I fucking love your cock," she yelled. "Fuck me harder!"

He did as he was told and pounded her so hard she moved up the mattress and had to push back from the headboard. When she did, his cock hit an even deeper spot inside her.

"Fuck me!" she screamed as she started pushing against his rhythm and the bed rocked itself back to the wall with loud, hard bursts.

"I'm gonna come," he screamed as they fucked so hard and fast she thought they were going to break the fucking bed.

"I'm coming again!" she yelled.

The bed slammed the wall as he fucked her wildly, giving her one final hard slap on the ass as they both came with dizzying pleasure.

"Fill me up baby," she screamed.

"I'm fucking filling you with my come," he panted.

He thrust one last time and then slowed his pace as they both started to come down from the high. He slowly slid out of her and laid down beside her as she collapsed flat on the mattress and let its cool silk relax her.

"Fuck," she said softly.

"Yeah," he agreed.

She glanced at him as he turned his head to her. "You're beautiful," he said quietly.

It made her laugh how sincere he was. This young man fresh out of college was sweet. He hadn't had his heart broken yet, not really, but he'd likely broken a few hearts with those icy blue eyes.

"Thank you," she said quietly.

"Are you doing this because of your divorce?" he asked. He smiled at her like he knew what this was

all about and just wanted her to say
it.

"What if I told you it was?" she
asked quietly.

"I'd be okay with it," he said. He
grinned widely and they both
laughed. "I mean, just be honest
with me. And we're good."

She nodded and let out a slow
exhale as she raised herself onto
her elbows. She gave him her best
smile.

"My ex and I. We really never
should have gotten married in the
first place," she said.

"Ah," he said. "Too young?"

"Too young," she replied. "And
we both made mistakes. But it still
hurts like a mother fucker no matter
who did what to whom."

She locked eyes with him, and
he nodded. He was so hot and yet,
she could tell, there was a lot
underneath those eyes. A lot more

than maybe most people gave him credit for. Including her.

"This is just sex for me, yes," she said quietly. And it really was. He was hot, and she liked him, but she already knew better than to get involved with a twenty-six-year-old. "It feels good. It makes me happy. And it's helping me move on. Are you okay with that?"

She tried to read his expression, but it seemed like he was pretty good at hiding his emotions. Whatever he was thinking, he finally arrived at a nod.

"I'm okay with that," he said. He slid across the bed and gave her a light kiss. "Roll on your side."

"What?" she asked.

"Roll on your side," he ordered. He nodded for her to face the other direction. She did as she was told and smiled at the little thrill it gave her. But the thrill she felt when he slid right up against her body and then pulled her into a close snuggle was even more electrifying.

"Does this feel good?" he whispered quietly in her ear.

"Yes," she whispered back.

"Good," he said. "I hope this helps you know how fucking gorgeous you are."

She was rendered speechless as they lay there in peace with the breeze from the open windows caressing their naked bodies.

She didn't know what to make of this moment, but she was trying very hard not to make more of it than it was. It was just a crazy sexual experience helping her through her divorce, and he was being nice. Right?

As her eyelids fluttered into a cozy sleep, she decided to believe just that.

And only that.

5

Missionary Means More

When Gina had walked into the bedroom naked two weeks ago and got on all fours, he'd almost come in his pants. It wasn't just that her body was lithe and curvy with the most perfectly waxed and pink pussy he'd ever seen, it was the expression on her face. Heady with desire and ready for whatever he had to give her.

And he had given her everything. They damn near broke the bed and he experienced a climax like he'd never had before. After that, she had been honest with where she was in this thing, that it was casual, to help her through her divorce. Exactly what he had thought, too.

But then her face.

Something in her eyes, when she was talking, had spoken to his insides. All he wanted to do in that moment was pull her close and hold on to her. He had seen on her face that she wanted him to agree with her, that this was nothing, so he did. But he wasn't about to leave that bed without holding her in his arms.

Then they had fallen asleep together and woke up later that afternoon, had incredible sex again, and they'd been fucking ever since. Never missionary, though, she wouldn't allow it.

"It's too personal," she had said. "Missionary means more."

And she'd gone down on him and sucked his cock so good he came almost immediately.

And now, it was his final day on the job, almost dark, and he would be leaving shortly. The new hardwood floor in her bedroom looked gorgeous, the bathroom was perfection, and the paint had dried to a beautiful shade of pearl that really opened the space. She had also brought in new photos and hung them or framed them, decorated with pillows and green plants, and made the whole space warm with soft, neutral fabrics.

It's exactly what he would have done. Especially the plants. She was good at the interior design aspect, and he had told her that a few times already.

"You're just saying that because we're fucking," she had quipped.

"I'm not," he said earnestly. "You're good at it. Have you ever considered it as your job?"

She had shrugged then and looked away.

"What?" he had pressed.

"I did think about it. In college," she had said quietly.

"What happened?"

"Blaine happened." She had laughed. "And I thought, I'm gonna be a wife, why do I need a fancy degree? So, I majored in business to help him with *his* business."

"Oh," he had replied quietly. "I see."

"It paid off, I guess," she had said. She shrugged with a smirk. "I did get a percentage of the business in the divorce. The percentage I helped him build, which he had no problem with. He knew I deserved it, so."

She had almost immediately kissed him then to change the subject. They hadn't spoken about it since.

Now, it was his last day on the job, and he could feel in his gut that he didn't want to leave her quite yet. He had gotten used to seeing her almost every day, to feeling her body next to his, to sliding deep inside her and knowing what made her come.

"Fuck," he whispered. His cock was immediately hard thinking about her. He knew this meant more than just a simple, casual relationship. At least to him.

"Whatcha thinkin' about?" she asked. She strode into the bedroom in little white shorts and a simple pink tank top that showed off her ample curves. Her long dark hair was cascading around her, and she looked much happier and lighter than when he'd knocked on her door almost four weeks ago.

"You," he said.

She smiled as she slid onto the bed and laid on her side, propping her head up with her hand.

"Oh yeah?" she asked quietly. "What about me?"

He walked up to her and kissed her gently as she let out a soft little moan. It drove him crazy when she made that noise. Like a little sex kitten and he was the only one who had what she needed.

"You like that?" he asked quietly.

"Mmm-hmmm," she murmured.

He reached down and un-did her shorts, sliding his fingers between her legs as she opened them for him. She was already slick and ready as his fingers teased her slit.

"Wet for me already?" He smiled at her as she grinned.

"Yes, baby." She reached up and kissed him.

When she pulled back, he did, too, at her protest. He smiled and walked away, going to the fireplace and lighting it up. It was a cool, summer evening as the sun finally set and the warmth from the fireplace was nice. He grabbed a couple pillows and a blanket and threw them on the fluffy rug in front of the fire.

"Come here," he directed.

She shook her head with a little smile.

"I said, come here," he ordered.

That did the trick. She loved it when he took control of her in the bedroom, and he had no problem with that. As she walked toward him, she stripped off her clothing, down to the bare-naked skin, beautiful and tan. He undressed as well and watched her expression as she took in his rock-hard body and his huge cock that was ready and waiting for her.

"Fuck baby," she said. She reached out and wrapped her small hand around his cock and started stroking his throbbing member.

"Mmmm," he grunted. "Fuck."

"How do you want me, baby?" she asked. "On my knees?"

"On your back."

"What?" She glanced at him in surprise. "No mission—"

"Gina," he interrupted. "I want you on your back so I can kiss you."

He leaned in then, grabbing the back of her hair with one hand and her perfect ass with the other. Then he dove into her neck and started kissing up it.

"And look in your eyes." He kissed up her chin.

"And touch your magnificent breasts." He slid his hand from her ass to her breasts and started thumbing her nipples.

"And watch you come while my cock drives deep inside you."

He kissed her then and when he did, he meant it. He didn't give a shit if he was twenty-six and she was thirty. Big fucking deal. He wanted her. And he wanted more than this. And now she knew that, too.

She pulled away quickly.

"Wolfe, I—"

"Gina," he interrupted again. "I
don't want this to end. I don't care
that I'm younger than you. This is
stupid. Let's just try. Please."

She paused for a second as he
held her stare, his thumb gently
caressing her nipple, his other hand
wrapped in her hair.

"You can say no," he said
quietly. "But just know that's not
what I want."

He slid his hands down and
around her back, letting her go a
little bit, but when he did, she slid
her arms up his and around his
neck, pulling him close to her.

"Can we take it slow?"

He was certain his grin was
bigger than it should be, but he
didn't care. He already cared about
this woman more than he ever
expected to and he wanted to
explore it and see what it was. The
fact she was game to even try was
enough for him.

"I can do that," he said quietly.

She smiled back at him and for the first time since this thing had started, he saw a bit of her guard drop. And behind it was a beautiful pair of honest, giving hazel eyes that he was getting lost in.

"You're gorgeous," he whispered.

She kissed him then and slowly slid down his body onto the rugs and blankets and pillows. She laid on her back and got comfortable, spreading her legs, and sliding one toe up his bare leg.

"Come here, baby," she whispered.

His heart skipped a beat as he got down on his knees and laid between her legs. The way his chest felt pressed against hers as he leaned down and kissed her was indescribable. They wrapped their arms around each other and rolled slightly to the side as her legs wrapped his back and his hands explored her body.

He opened his eyes and kissed her lightly as she opened hers. His lips grazed hers as the gaze between them heated to an impossible temperature.

"I want you so bad," he whispered.

"Then take me," she whispered back.

He stared in her eyes and reached down to her leg, opening it wider as he slid his fingers inside of her and rubbed her wet folds.

"Yes," she moaned.

He ran his fingers up and down her slick lips then stopped at her clit and mercilessly circled and rubbed it until she was panting.

"Fuck, Wolfe, yes," she panted.

He dipped his head down and pulled her nipple into his mouth as he slid his fingers deep inside her. She moaned so loud he grinned.

God, this is all he wanted. To make her happy.

"Wolfe, fuck me, please," she begged.

"Beg me," he directed.

"Please, baby, please," she begged. "Slide your beautiful cock inside me. Make me yours. Own my pussy, baby."

The words made him so hard he could barely contain himself as he positioned himself at her entrance and gazed into her eyes.

"You're so fucking beautiful," he whispered as he gazed in her eyes. She gave him nothing but happiness back.

"You're making me rethink everything," she whispered.

"Good," he said quietly.

He slowly inserted his tip as she moaned with pleasure.

"Yes," she breathed. "Deeper."

"Yes, baby," he said.

He slid deeper and deeper.

"Fuck yes, baby," she panted.
"All the way. Please."

He thrust all the way in as she
wrapped her legs around his back.
It took only a second before they
found a rhythm and their hips were
rocking against each other in
perfect fashion. Her wetness all
over his cock and balls as they beat
steadily against her perfect ass.

"Harder, baby," she ordered.

"Yes, baby," he said. He thrust
harder and harder as he kissed her
deeply and ran his hand over her
breasts.

"I'm gonna come," she moaned.
"Baby, I'm gonna come."

He looked into her eyes then and
saw the pleasure. It was all he
wanted. This moment with her. It
was perfect.

"I'm coming, too," he panted.
"Fuck, baby, fuck."

They pushed each other to the
edge in a swift fashion as their

orgasms came fast and strong. He pushed deep inside her and stayed there for a second as they both caught their breath and hs come filled her.

He slowly pulled out and looked in her eyes, kissing her gently until their breathing slowed.

"That was perfect," he whispered.

She laughed. "As long as you realize I'm not perfect."

He kissed her again. "Agreed.. As long as you realize I'm not perfect, either.

She smiled at him. "Agreed."

They kissed gently like that for a few moments, before Wolfe rolled them both onto their sides, face-to-face.

"So, how about a real first date?" he asked.

She laughed. "Oh God."

She tucked a hair behind her ear and looked in his eyes. "Are we really gonna do this then?"

She searched his eyes as he smiled.

"We're really gonna do this," he said.

She twitched her lips, a habit she had when she was thinking about something and preparing to make a decision. He'd seen her do it about fifty times during this renovation.

"Okay," she agreed quietly.

"So," he said. "First date?"

"First date," she said quietly.

He kissed her lightly. "Good."

He wrapped his arms around her, and they fell asleep just like that.

.

6

Business or Pleasure?

Wolfe could feel his former teammates and now co-business partners staring him down. None of them moved or said a thing. Finally, Mr. GQ himself spoke.

"So, hang on," Danny said slowly. Of course, his childhood friend would be the first to weigh in as he rubbed his face then looked straight at Wolfe. "So, this is a relationship, then?"

Wolfe shrugged. "I mean, it's not *not* a relationship. But it also is."

"That…makes perfect sense, sure," Ben quipped. He shrugged with a laugh as Jack cracked up.

"Yeah, man, clear as mud," Jack added.

They all laughed a little as Wolfe grinned.

"I know, it sounds stupid," Wolfe said. "But I can't help it. I like her. I do. She's…I don't know. She's got something."

"Yeah, a perfect ass and tits," Danny said sarcastically.

"No, no," Wolfe said. He shook his head. "Don't talk about her like that."

"Ohhhhh," Jack said as he sat up, followed quickly by Ben.

"Oh shit," Ben said. "You got the 'don't talk about her like that' speech."

Ben pointed at Danny who looked surprised.

"Damn son," Danny cracked. "Okay, you do like her then."

Wolfe could feel the blush move across his cheeks. He did like her. He didn't necessarily want these assholes to know how much just yet, but…too late. He'd shown his hand.

"So, when's the first date?" Jack asked.

"This weekend," Wolfe said.

"Where ya takin' her?" Danny asked.

"I'm not sure," Wolfe said with a shrug. "I want it to be special, but not too special, ya know?"

They all nodded. They knew what that meant. The beginning of a relationship. You don't want to start too fast or seem too eager. But you also don't want to seem like you're not trying. Especially with a woman like Gina. Who had been down the marriage road and knew shit. She was older, wiser, and clued in a lot more to the little things and what they meant. Plus, she had made it perfectly clear she wanted to go slow. He needed to respect that.

"Hey, what about that little dive down on Harding Street?" Danny asked.

"Oh yeah," Ben agreed. "That place would be perfect."

"Agreed," Jack said. "It's a dive, so it's casual, but the food and the environment are intimate and amazing, bringing it up a notch. Perfect balance you're looking for."

Wolfe nodded. His buddies were right. And since they knew he was into this woman, they wouldn't steer him wrong.

"I like it," Wolfe said. "Love it, actually. She'll love it, too."

"Cool," Danny said. His friend eyed him for a second. "Good for you, man. You look happy."

"Thanks." Wolfe nodded with a smile.

"Okay, bigger problem, though," Jack said.

"What's that?" Ben asked.

"So, your little escapade has yielded some results," Jack said as they all turned to him. "Your girl has been singing your praises. In the form of twenty-seven messages. All women. All ages. Looking for renovations."

"Twenty-seven?" Danny asked. He glanced at Wolfe. "Well done, man."

They all cracked up.

"So, wait, what if these women expect sex as part of the renovation?" Ben asked. "Legit, is that prostitution?"

"We're not, no," Danny said. He shook his head. "Wolfe's situation is not typical and it's not going to become typical. No sex on the job."

They all looked at him.

"Well, not for money, anyway," Danny said. They all laughed.

"So, what do we ask when we do the quote? Do we make sure it's legit?" Wolfe asked.

"Business or pleasure?" Jack asked.

"Business first," Danny said. "And then, well, maybe pleasure."

They all nodded in agreement as they started to work the list of twenty-seven messages and doling out the assignments.

Business was well underway.

And maybe, just maybe, a little bit of pleasure.

<u>**More to Come!**</u>

Wolfe's sexy story isn't over! Keep reading the *Men Who Renovate Erotic Series* to see what happens to him, Gina, and his sexy friends! Wanna learn more about the other men—Danny, Jack, and Ben? Keep reading the *Men Who Renovate Erotic Series* as they build their business, enjoy sex, and talk about it all!

Scan me

<u>**Review this book!**</u>

Do you love *Master of the Bedroom* as part of the *Men Who Renovate Erotic Series*? Then tell everyone about it! Leave a review on Amazon.com!